6/18

DATE DUE

The Library Store #47-0119

D1164729

Do Princesses Live in Sandcastles?

Carmela LaVigna Coyle

Pictures by Mike Gordon

Guilford, Connecticut

Published by Muddy Boots
An imprint of The Rowman & Littlefield Publishing Group, Inc.
4501 Forbes Blvd., Ste. 200
Lanham, MD 20706
www.rowman.com

MuddyBootsBooks.com

Distributed by NATIONAL BOOK NETWORK

British Library Cataloguing-in-Publication Information available

Library of Congress Control Number: 2017962766

ISBN 978-1-63076-296-4 (hardcover)

ISBN 978-1-63076-297-1 (e-book)

Printed in Yuanzhou, China
May 2018

To children everywhere and every splish-splashing moment.
—clvc

The many hours spent on the beach with my grandkids Caiden and Carter this summer
have left me with a lifetime of memories of the fun you can have buried on the beach!
—M.G.

Do princesses spend the whole day at the shore?

The beach is a marvelous place to explore.

What kind of creature
made these tracks in the sand?

They're made by sea turtles
who nest on the land.

Why do the waves seem to stop at the beach?

I think that's as far as the ocean can reach.

Does a princess build sandcastles with shovels and pails?

I brought extra tools for those minor details.

Does a princess ride on a purple seahorse?

With a dolphin in tow, then I say of course!

Seagulls have been circling for almost an hour.

They're on the lookout for fish to devour.

When a princess goes snorkeling does she HAVE to wear fins?

Well, that's when her job as a mermaid begins.

What do those hermit crabs have on their backs?

They carry their homes like giant backpacks.

Does a princess get sand between all of her toes?

You'd be surprised all the places it goes.

Watch me catch waves on my new boogie board.

Your epic attempts deserve an award.

How in the world will we EVER spot whales?

Let's sit on this hill and watch for their tails.

How does this shell make the sound of the sea?

THAT *has always been a mystery to me.*

Are princesses strong and enormously brave?

They stand at the edge and shout, "Bring it on, WAVE!"

Why does the ocean make that glittery light?

They stand at the edge and shout, "Bring it on, WAVE!"

Why does the ocean make that glittery light?

It comes when the sun hits the ripples just right.

Sparkle
like the ocean!